Not
Opposites

Not better. Not worse. Just different.

Written by **Linda Ragsdale**

Illustrated by **Imodraj**

Always remember to
show love, choose peace,
and see the beauty in
the world around you.

Designed by Flowerpot Press in Franklin, TN.
www.FlowerpotPress.com
Designer: Stephanie Meyers
Editor: Katrine Crow
ROR-0808-0101
ISBN: 978-1-4867-1255-7
Made in China/Fabriqué en Chine

There is nothing a Peace Dragon likes better than teaching and learning about peace.

Sometimes differences are not better or worse, or opposites; they're just different. We learn how they can work together for the same goal in the pages of this book.

So come on inside...it's peaceful in here.

Wings.

Arms.

Not better.
Not worse.
Not opposites.
Just different.

Webbed feet.

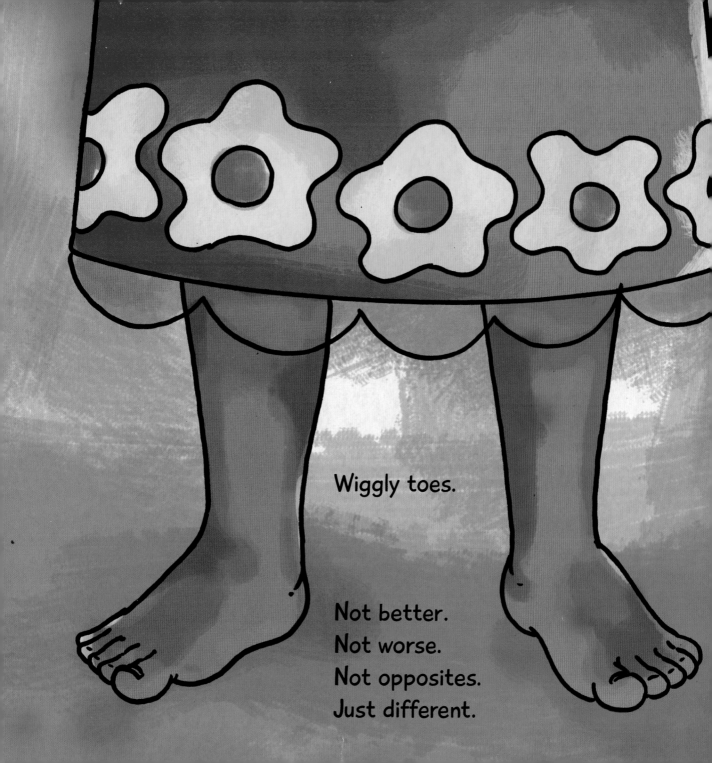

Wiggly toes.

Not better.
Not worse.
Not opposites.
Just different.

Beak.

Mouth.

Not better.
Not worse.
Not opposites.
Just different.

Nose.

Snout.

Hair.

Fur.

Hands.

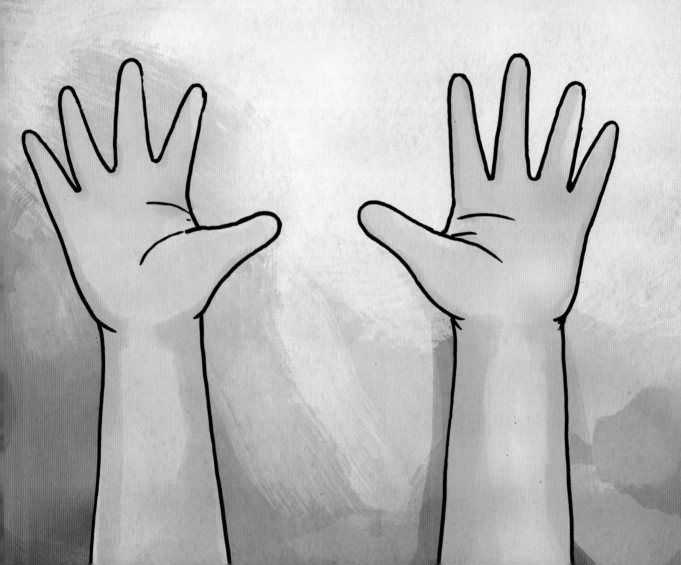

Him.

Different parts for different purposes.
Not better.
Not worse.

Not opposites.
Just different.

Strong.

Tall.

Better for some.
Not better for all.
Just different.

Different is you.
Different is me.
Together, differences work.

Together, but different.
Just right.

Hi! I'm Pax. I'm a Peace Dragon.

My very favorite thing in the entire world is to fly around the world and encourage people to be peacemakers, like in these books. Did you know that everyone can be a peacemaker? If you choose to see, speak, and act through a kind heart and calm thoughts, YOU are a peacemaker! Once you practice, it's easy—and pretty fun, too!

We all have times where we need help choosing peace, such as learning to work with people who are different than we are, or dealing with unkind words that come our way. By reading and thinking about ways to choose kindness or peace before a challenge comes our way, it helps us be prepared to choose peace.

By practicing awesome peaceful solutions, we become examples of love, while building a foundation of peacemaking that will last a lifetime.

Pax